Runaway Baby Brother

by Katy Hudson

Random House New York

For my nephews,
Thomas and William,
for being my
constant source
of inspiration.

And for their dad,
Kib, my honorary
brother.

Copyright © 2018 by Katy Hudson

All rights reserved. Published in the United States by
Random House Children's Books,
a division of Penguin Random House LLC, New York.

Random House and the colophon are registered
trademarks of Penguin Random House LLC.

Visit us on the Web! randomhousekids.com

Educators and librarians, for a variety of teaching tools,
visit us at RHTeachersLibrarians.com

Library of Congress Cataloging-in-Publication Data
is available upon request.

ISBN 978-1-5247-1860-2 (trade) —
ISBN 978-1-5247-1861-9 (lib. bdg.) —
ISBN 978-1-5247-1862-6 (ebook)

MANUFACTURED IN CHINA

10 9 8 7 6 5 4 3 2 1

First Edition

Random House Children's Books supports the
First Amendment and celebrates the right to read.

Chick had been told getting a new baby brother would be great.
He didn't agree.

Peep!

Chick couldn't go anywhere or do anything without his baby brother being there too.

Peep!

Peep!

"He's *always* there!" complained Chick.

"He loves you and just wants to be with his big brother,"
explained Mama Hen.

But Baby Brother couldn't do anything. . . .

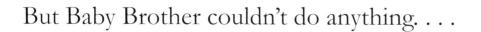

"No, you need to
stand over there."

"Right . . . catch."

"Right . . . throw. . . .
Ugh, it's all slobbery!"

He couldn't jump.

SHEEP
PEN

Wool
for Sale

He couldn't play any of Chick's favorite games. "Three, two, one! Ready or not, here I come!"

He couldn't even walk properly . . .

. . . because his baby diaper got in the way.
What a nuisance!

Worst of all, he cried all the time.

HEN COOP

"Finally," thought Chick. "Alone at last."

But then:

Peep.

"Ugh, why are you always there?"
cried Chick. "Look. Only big
chicks can climb trees.
Go home!"

Peep.

"Get lost!" Chick yelled.

Chick kept climbing to the top of the tree, leaving his little brother behind.

"Wooooo-hooooo!" he called,
and jumped to the pond below.

Chick splashed and played all afternoon. He had so much fun that he forgot about his annoying baby brother until the sun went down.

Chick stumbled along the darkened path to home.

As he made his way as quickly as he could,
Chick heard a rustling in the shadows.

"Who's there?"
Chick trembled. A fox? A wolf?

A ghost?

"Oh, it's just you!" said Chick, relieved.

"Probably best to walk home together."

As they walked home, Chick realized there was
one good thing about having a baby brother. . . .

He was always there.